Why I Love My Daddy

Illustrated by Daniel Howarth

HarperCollins *Children's Books*

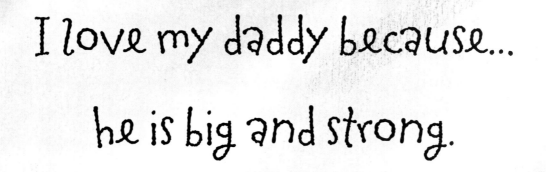

I love my daddy because...
he is big and strong.

I love my daddy because...

he is clever.

I love my daddy because...

he keeps me safe and cosy.

I love my daddy because...

he carries me.

I love my daddy because...

he is handsome.

I love my daddy because...

he is funny.

I love my daddy because...

he hugs me good night.

I love my daddy because...

he fixes things.

I love my daddy because...

he is kind.

I love my daddy because...

he is my best friend.

Everyone loves their daddy,

First published in hardback in Great Britain by HarperCollins *Children's Books* in 2006
This edition published in 2020

1 3 5 7 9 10 8 6 4 2

978-0-00-798395-7

HarperCollins *Children's Books* is a division of HarperCollins*Publishers* Ltd.

Text and illustrations copyright © HarperCollins*Publishers* Ltd 2006

A CIP catalogue record for this title is available from the British Library.
Visit our website at: www.harpercollins.co.uk

Printed and bound in China